XENTASTIC

THE FATE DIAMOND SERIES
BOOK 2

MAURY K. DOWNS

Xentastic

Adapted from the Jewel Sky Productions and Dirt Merchants Films
motion picture, Xentastic directed by Henning Morales
and based on the novel, The Way You See Me Now written by
Maury K. Downs

Published in the United States of America
By Jewel Sky Publications and Productions

THE LEGEND OF THE ALMASI YA KIFO DIAMONDS

Legend has it the Almasi Ya Kifo diamonds were discovered in Africa. Although, the exact origin is unknown. The supernatural powers of the diamonds are the compelling conversations of legend and cultural folklore. The animate power of the cosmos within the diamonds amplifies all the harmonic energy of the possessor. For example, the generous intentions of a kind-hearted person's goodwill can be intensified, protecting them from harm and positively affecting others around them. Conversely, individuals disreputable in character will find pronounced misfortune along their path while in custody of the stones. Especially if there is any malicious intent, such as the exploitation of the gems for greed or selfish covetousness.

In diverse cultures the mysterious gems are known as "Fate Diamonds" because of the wealth and good luck they are said to bestow. Although they can bring good luck, the diamonds are legendarily known for the peculiar misgivings and calamities that follow when possessing them. Hence, their notorious epithet, Almasi Ya Kifo. A lingo in Swahili meaning, "Death Diamonds". Nevertheless, the diamonds are considered priceless by many experts in the diamond industry. The gems are so rare and the legend such a mystique, that they are tirelessly sought after by many gem collectors – and those with greedy intent.

Certain ancient tribes around the world acknowledge that the diamonds hold supernatural powers and retain an energy beyond any comprehension. These are the tribes that have a profound belief regarding the danger of the stones. They are people sworn under armistice and primed through ritual to keep the stones safely hidden when they fall in their possession at any given time.

Myth or fact, magic or science? This can only be determined by the individual experiencing the diamond's intense affects when in their possession.

Dedicated to

Lorna, your love and support give me the passion
and strength to always succeed. Mahal Kita.

Mom, Dad, Ritha, Marcia, Michael, Ryan, Kristoffer, Jasmin,
Kristina, Gillian, Addison, Jaxon and Logan. You are all part of me.

The Xentastic Film

Producing a film during the COVID-19 pandemic was definitely not an easy task. Through the professionalism, determination, and hard work of the cast and crew, we managed to successfully navigate through the additional health and safety requirements. To everyone who worked on the film project, you have our grateful and heartfelt thanks. The final result could not have been any better. The Xentastic film has surpassed our hopes and to date has won many film festival awards:

8 & Halfilm Awards 2023
Best Narrative Feature, Best Producer

Roswell Sci-Fi Film Fest 2022
Best Short Film

Focus International Film Festival 2022
Best Feature Film, Best Lead Actress, Best Lead Actor,
Best Supporting Actress, Best Supporting Actor,
Best Feature Film Trailer, Best Film Poster

L.A. Sci-Fi & Horror Festival 2022
Best Picture, Best Music Track

The Great Canadian Sci-Fi Film Festival 2022
Best Actress

Directed by Henning Morales

Music by Drew Lane

Producers: Jeff McGrail, Barbara Lynn, Maury K. Downs,
Lorna Downs

Starring: Sylvia Van Hoeven, Jonathan Platero

Co-starring: Reyna Calvo, Lex Night

Featuring: Ari Lagomarsino, Jerry Boyd, Alan D. Waserman,
Dennis Sanchez, Roberta De Santis

On set during the filming of Xentastic

Producers Maury and Lorna Downs

Maury Downs and
Jonathan Platero (Spencer)

Lorna Downs and
Sylvia Van Hoeven (Xen)

ABOUT THE AUTHOR

Maury K. Downs was born and raised in Los Angeles, California. He has had a rewarding previous career working as a health care provider. His joy is all things aviation, and he is a certificated pilot and flight instructor. He has traveled the world as an airline transport pilot. He holds a type rating in the "Queen of the skies" Boeing 747 and the Airbus 320. When he was a child, he enjoyed telling imaginary stories to his friends and family for their entertainment. He enjoys hearing the humorous cavorts and bold adventures of people's travels. "The Way You See Me Now" was his debut novel, and it is the prelude to this exciting book series.

CHAPTER 1
ONE TOO MANY

Monday, October 1st, 2001

IT'S A BEAUTIFUL sunny morning in Tuscany, Italy. Xenyatta Davenport (Xen to those that know her) is parked along a lonely, quiet stretch of road near the Accona desert. She is patiently waiting, ready to complete a secret delivery.

Why the secrecy? While Xen is a well-known fashion model and has graced the covers of many magazines, she also has a covert and ultra-confidential side profession; transporting precious gems for insurance companies.

Xen had arrived into Italy a couple of days earlier on a flight from Los Angeles International Airport. A hire car was ready for her and her hotel accommodations are first-rate, both of which her anonymous employer had previously arranged. She has had time to relax and take a walk around town, doing a little sightseeing on her own. She is enjoying her trip. Everything is going nicely according to plan.

Xen looks at the two jewelry boxes that are currently hidden in a trendy white tote bag. It is the same white tote she had received on Saturday in the airport terminal from another contracted transporter, a beautiful older woman.

Suddenly her phone rings. The call is from an unlisted number. She exclaims, "That's the third time since I landed creep!" Looking at her phone, she says, "Show your number or mommy doesn't answer!" She ends the unwanted call.

Then another car pulls up and parks facing Xen's vehicle. Xen grabs the tote bag, opens the door, and gets out of the car. It's time for business.

A young woman exits the other car from the back passenger seat and starts to walk towards Xen. As they get closer Xen sees it is the glamorous and well-dressed, Francesca Conti, her contact in Italy.

"Why are we meeting out here?" Xen inquires sulkily.

"We need to be extra careful these days. I want to make sure you weren't followed." Francesca retorts.

"My employers are insurance companies, not gangsters like your team, back in the day. My runs are legit." Xen smirks and looks around. "Isn't this a bit much?"

"It used to be the cops and robbers we had to look out for. Now it's just the robbers. These packages are much more valuable than ever. So, your employers asked us on the receiving end to be extra careful." Francesca makes no excuse for the seclusion.

"Are these headed for a museum or an expo?" Xen assumes the reason for the delivery method and all the quiet concealment.

"Even if I did know, you know I couldn't tell you."

Xen shrugs her shoulders and hands Francesca the tote bag. Francesca opens it and pulls out one of jewelry cases. She examines it, nods to Xen and hands the tote bag back to Xen. "Enjoy your stay in Tuscany." Francesca turns to walk away.

"No. There's another one." Xen exclaims.

"Pardon?" Francesca turns back around looking very confused and says, "This is the delivery. It's all here."

"I'm telling you, there's another." Xen looks around nervously. She reaches into the bag and pulls out the other identical box and hands it to Francesca.

Francesca is not expecting this. Very curiously, she opens the box. And to her absolute astonishment, revealed are the most accursed jewels she has ever set eyes on or heard about. Francesca's expression immediately changes from solemn to terrified at sight of the glimmering blueish diamonds. She fearfully snaps the case closed and yells and screams in her native Italian tongue. "Riprendilo!" Her eyes are wide and panicked. "Take it back, take it back, Almasi Ya Kifo! Almasi Ya Kifo!" She thrusts the case back into Xen's hands. "Where did you get it?! Who gave that to you? Where did you get it?!"

"The same as always. It was in the tote I received at the airport handover. What's wrong Francesca?" Xen hasn't the slightest clue as to why she is carrying on so.

"Fortuna mortale, diamanti della morte!" Francesca is rambling. "I never saw those!" She fiercely exclaims to Xen.

"Huh?"

"I never saw those stones. I want to hear you say it!"

"You never saw those stones." Xen replies as requested.

Francesca, visibly flustered, turns and signals to her driver. She gets in and the car hastily drives off.

Xen watches for a moment. Then she turns around and walks back towards her hire car, dumbfounded.

What happened? Why the extra case? Then she remembers the strange encounter in the airport terminal before she boarded her flight. A clumsy young man had literally run into her. He must have quickly stashed the case into her bag, but Xen, sitting stunned on the floor, hadn't noticed. *He had seemed such a kind stranger too.*

CHAPTER 2
FRIED CHICKEN

SPENCER CORRADO IS sleeping comfortably in his large bed, alone. The city lights of metro Los Angeles are shimmering through the massive modern windows of his high-rise, upscale apartment.

Then, suddenly he wakes up. He hears a noise coming from one of the other rooms and the lights are flickering on and off. He looks at the clock next to his bed. It's 3:00 AM. He gets up and cautiously opens the bedroom door. Spencer relaxes and smiles. The mysterious noises are coming from the kitchen, from his new girlfriend, Xen. She is sitting there in the dark, with her back towards him.

Xen had arrived from her overseas assignment yesterday. They had shared a delicious home cooked meal prepared by Spencer. Then they had watched one of Spencer's documentary films for a television project he's working on. He thought she had gone home, so is somewhat surprised to see her. He smiles as he starts to walk towards where Xen is sitting.

Xen is staring out the window gazing up at the starlit night sky, her eyes blinking rapidly. Bones from three pieces of fried chicken she has eaten lay on her plate as evidence of her ravenous hunger, picked clean. Spencer turns on a low light. She slowly turns to Spencer, drumstick in hand. With a juicy mouthful of fried chicken and still chewing, Xen says "I like your apartment." She raises her eyebrows in affirmation.

Spencer takes a moment to process all this. The situation seems such a dichotomy to the way Xen usually appears and acts. Holding a greasy piece of chicken in the same hands she wears her platinum bangle bracelet and Gucci folding clasp watch. He chuckles and shakes his head in amusement as he looks her over. Xen, so stylish in her little designer Y2K fashion dress and high heels. She's quirky and cute. And he likes that.

He smiles at his unconventional fashion model girlfriend as he sits close to her. "Geez, you're mauling that chicken like there was a prize in it for you at the bottom of that box."

Xen shrugs it off.

"How are you so skinny?" Spencer candidly inquires.

"What? I'm hungry. It's all there was."

He laughs, amused and intrigued. She eats. Spencer notices Xen's phone and sees there are several missed calls. Just at that moment, the apartment lights flicker again and the phone rings silently. The display shows, No Caller ID.

Xen ignores the call and casually throws her phone into her bag, saying, "I gotta go. Call me tomorrow?"

"You gotta go? Where?" Spencer raises his hands slightly. Xen is consumed with the chicken, finishing the last piece. "You never told me about your trip. You don't even seem tired."

She finally responds, nonchalantly. "Nothing to tell really. Flashing bulbs, flamboyant designers, champagne dinners, pretty boring, really." She grabs her purse, ready to head out.

Spencer, as if his attempt at amicable conversation will halt her departure says, "Did you visit anywhere interesting, see friends?"

"I really like you, Spencer. I have a feeling that this can go somewhere, but you gotta stop with the interrogation. You have nothing to be jealous about." She bats her eyes at him.

"I'm not jealous, really. It's been a couple months and I know very little about you, that's all." Spencer says, trying his best not to sound like he is pleading and prodding right now. "I didn't even know you liked chicken."

"Is that it? You want me to stop eating chicken?" She demurely quips with a slight glance at him.

He chuckles, sincerely charmed by her witty sex appeal. "I don't care about the chicken."

She still has chicken grease on her face. But before Spencer can say anything else, Xen embraces her grinning boyfriend and kisses him squarely on the mouth. Xen has an incomparable sensational kiss. Spencer is in Heaven right now. "Magic kiss." He says and grins. She smiles. She wipes her mouth. He wipes his. She stuffs the box into the garbage and grabs her purse. The lights flicker again as she struts out. Spencer's face changes to a more solemn expression as he watches Xen shut the apartment door behind her. *Why are the lights flickering?*

CHAPTER 3
CAN'T STOP THINKING ABOUT THE CHICKEN

LATE WEDNESDAY MORNING Spencer and his close friend Brock Vorster are playing basketball on the outdoor courts at Newport Beach in Orange County. It's a beautiful day to be outside. Spencer can't help but talk about Xen. "I can't stop thinking about the chicken man." He's standing at the free-throw line with the basketball, poised for a shot.

"Will you shut up about the chicken already, you sound like a freak." Brock teases.

"Bro, you should have seen it. I wake up..." Spencer is making gestures like he's eating his hand.

Brock promptly interrupts his longtime friend. Spencer has mentioned these details more than once already. "I know, I know. You wake up at three in the morning and think the space invaders are raiding your kitchen, and it's Xen eating chicken. So what? You gotta stop with all that alien science fiction nonsense." Brock waves his hand and shakes his head.

"She has a drumstick in her hand, her teeth sunk in it, feasting. She looked like a lion on the Serengeti tearing the skin and guts off a gazelle or some shit." Spencer does an impression of that, gesturing with his hands. He is trying his best to look serious, but his buddy just continues to chuckle aloud.

"So, she's a sloppy eater." Brock shrugs his shoulders.

"That's just it. She's not. At dinner she's always dainty as hell... uses all the right forks, takes small bites, sips her wine, ladylike." Spencer is now imitating all of that.

"So what, Spencer? What of it?" Brock raises his eyebrows.

"You introduced us. What more can you tell me?" Spencer earnestly inquires in a less humorous tone of voice now.

"I don't know her that well." Brock shrugs, thinking.

"How did you meet again?" Spencer holds the basketball at his side, trying to remember what Brock had told him before.

"My family's diamond business back in Cape Town." Brock shares what he remembers with a little more detail this time. "She was doing a photoshoot for a jewelry company my father supplies to. What are you getting at?"

"She leaves for days on end on these photo shoots but... it seems like she hasn't been in anything really big in a while."

"Look man, she's hot as the sun, she's fun and quirky. She's into you. Don't ask me why." He points at his buddy, Spencer, saying sternly, "Don't screw this up, man." Spencer raises the ball for a free throw shot. They go back to playing basketball.

CHAPTER 4
SUPERNATURAL POWERS

MEANWHILE, NOT FAR away, Xen is leaving the Santa Monica Public Library with a book she finds interesting. She has been there most of the morning, researching out of curiosity. She searched for anything relevant regarding the mysterious diamonds that she still has in her possession. *Why did Francesca react the way she did when she opened the jewelry case?* Xen recollected vividly the look of terror in Francesca's eyes. A profound reaction that gives Xen motivation to learn more about the legend of the Almasi Ya Kifo diamonds. *What had Francesca heard about them? What is it about these diamonds that make them so terrible?*

Xen reasons, if she doesn't look at the cursed stones, she won't be affected by them. Befitting, because Xen never opens a box, folder, or anything given to her by her covert employers during a transport. She has been specifically instructed to never look at the goods. Never put yourself in a position to be tempted or disloyal. Never get yourself personally involved was policy. Sticking to this rule, she never considered opening the jewelry case containing the Almasi Ya Kifo diamonds. Not once.

Less than half an hour later Xen is walking towards a perfect location she has spotted on the beach. She loves that it is a beautiful day for it. Her natural long blonde hair is tied up in a ponytail and she has taken her boots off so her toes can feel the warm sand. She has a beach chair, water bottle, oversized purse, and book in hand.

It doesn't take long before she has made herself comfortable in her beach chair. The relaxing sound of the waves along the beautiful stretch of shoreline is her only companion now. Xen takes the book she just checked out and looks at the cover again: TRIBALISM OF SOUTH AFRICA AND NATIVE AMERICA. She opens the book to the page, LEGEND OF THE ALMASI YA KIFO GEMS. And she begins reading to herself.

The Indigenous people of Africa, Asia and the Americas have revered and feared the Almasi Ya Kifo diamonds that are also known as, Deadly Fortune. They acknowledge that the stones hold supernatural powers and retain an energy beyond any human comprehension. A great power that can influence destiny.

The diamonds are a shared proprietorship between specific tribes at specific longitude and latitudes, mainly in three parts of the world. One location, controversially believed to be the origin of the stones, is in South Africa. Another area is in Australia and, there is another significant location in Lake Arrowhead, California, USA.

Legend has it that the native people use the stones in their rituals, but they are never traded. They should not be permanently taken away from the tribal chiefs' dwellings and are passed down through the generations.

The stones possess a peculiar celebratory power, according to the legend. They are only exposed for special occasions of celebration and then hidden away for the next one.

When there are rumors of a potential attack on the tribe, the jewels are entrusted with the kindest of hearts for safekeeping. This person must not be connected with the tribe in any way, thus ensuring the safety of the precious gems from enemies. However, holders of the gems that have not been entrusted be warned of the misfortune and misgivings to follow. The gems are often sought after, because of their exceptional value. On the open market each diamond could be worth up to a million dollars.

Xen smiles as she remembers how easily she persuaded the customs agents on her return trip to the United States about the gems being prototype costume jewelry for a new brand. She remembers how the agents seemed lost in thought and allowed her to clear through without another word. *Supernatural powers?* She chuckles.

Xen is convinced that she is now the holder of the stones she is reading about. She gives it another thought, legend of them bringing bad luck and such. Although she has not found exact instances involving possessing or looking at the stones, Xen figures hearsay is evidence enough. There must be something bad about them, otherwise people wouldn't have anything to say about such things.

Now, regarding her own wellbeing, Xen isn't worried the slightest. She feels confident some fabled damnation will not befall her, like something out of an Indiana Jones movie. On the contrary. For some strange reason she sincerely feels at peace holding onto the gems. Almost as if she was supposed to hold them for now. Why she is feeling this way is frankly unbeknown to her. It is just a reassuring feeling she has, deep inside.

She thinks of what to do next. Xen has no idea why she has been entrusted with them. But she figures it must be for some good reason. She is not interested in selling the diamonds, although she certainly believes what they are worth. She realizes the significance of the stones and what they must mean to the trusted peoples that keep them. Someone appointed and special probably relies on and need these diamonds. They must want them back.

Xen has told no one about the jewels. Francesca knows, but Xen also knows Francesca doesn't want to have anything to do with the diamonds. Francesca would certainly swear she never saw them, again. Oddly, Xen imagines someone significant must know the jewels are in her possession right now. Looking towards the heavens, she considers. *There is a greater power behind all this.*

CHAPTER 5
X FILES AND MARTINIS

LATER THAT WEDNESDAY Spencer is in his apartment sitting at his desk. He rubs his chin, deep in thought about the film project he is working on. There are a couple screenplays that are work in progress, and a notepad laid across the large desk in front of him. He lightly taps the pencil between his fingers on the desk as he thinks. Spencer sighs and leans back in his chair for a moment. Then he leans forward and places the pencil down next to a framed picture of him standing next to an FBI agent, who is Spencer's good friend. The picture is a large, reprinted cover of a recent edition of Hollywood Weekly Magazine. The article was for an event held in Anaheim, California a few months ago. The headline reads: Award Winning Writer, Director and Former FBI Agent Team Up – Film Director Spencer Corrado and Special Agent Horatio Mendez speak at the Youth Mentorship Forum.

Spencer gets up and moves to a more comfortable spot in his living room to relax. He wants to take a break from his work. He sits on the couch and opens a magazine. As soon as he begins reading, there is a knock at the door. Spencer gives a quick glance towards the apartment door and says, "It's open."

The FBI agent in the magazine cover photo, Horatio Mendez, enters. He is a handsome 60-year-old gentleman dressed business casual. Spencer is delighted as they greet each other as old friends do.

"What's so serious that we couldn't do this over the phone?" Mendez smiles at Spencer.

"We do our best work over martinis right here, Mendez." Spencer points toward the living room, gesturing for his good friend to sit comfortably.

"So, we're working?" Mendez quips with a chuckle.

"Get you a drink?" Spencer offers Mendez.

"Man, it's barely five." Mendez replies plopping himself down on the sofa. They laugh as Spencer prepares martinis.

Soon, there's another knock at the door. Spencer looks at Mendez. Spencer opens the door. It's Dolores Mendez, about sixteen years in age junior to her darling husband. She is very pretty, impeccably dressed, sophisticated, confident, witty, and known to be a little bitchy at times.

"I thought you were waiting in the car?" Mendez has his shoulder turned to look at her, cocktail in hand.

"And you said it was a quick stop, Horatio." She responds with raised eyebrows. "I'm not going to sit in the car like some Labrador while you drink martinis with the self-purported success guru, gabbing about old times. No offence Spencer." She nods playfully at her award-winning, writer director friend.

"None taken." Spencer kindly nods back. "How are you, Dolores?" He kisses her lightly on the cheek.

"Simply parched, darling. Mix me one of those, will ya?" She points at the large martini in her husband's hand.

Spencer grabs another glass and makes her a martini. He looks at Mendez, hesitant to continue their conversation.

Dolores breaks the awkward silence. "Oh, Spencer, now come on. What's the rumpus? You know you can say anything in front of me. Just because we don't see eye to eye on everything doesn't make me the enemy." Dolores receives and takes a generous sip of her dirty martini. Freshly prepared by Spencer with Beefeater London Dry Gin and three soaked Spanish Queen olives. As her lips part the crystal glass, her expression bears full satisfaction of the perfectly mixed dry cocktail.

"I don't know. This is kinda sensitive." Spencer gestures. But really intending, *you're here now, I can't.*

"Who gave you the idea about using the Kuklo blowing ritual of the Chamorros in the Guam Pacific Island for your last movie?" Dolores raises her chin.

"You did, Dolores." Spencer affirms.

"You wanted to use the legend of Babang Canyon. That would have been a mistake, right?" She asks straightforwardly.

"Yes, Dolores." He acknowledges.

"So, tell it like it is." She takes another sip.

Spencer queries with a smile, "Sworn to secrecy?" She crosses her heart. Then he directs his attention to Mendez, "You FBI guys are the ones that are supposed to be covering up all the alien landings and whatnot, right?"

"I wasn't part of that, you know, those X files investigations." Mendez replies. "In the Bureau, one department doesn't know what the other is doing, unless it's necessary. Nothing in the X files is necessary." He pouts, matter of fact.

"What do you think of Xen? You met her at the gala" Spencer asks with a slight raised brow.

"She's a real doll. Pretty, smart, sophisticated. What's not to love? She's perfect." Dolores replies, bringing her drink to her lips. The level in the martini glass has been receding at a steady pace.

"But isn't she a bit too perfect?" Spencer frankly poses.

"You trying to find flaws?" Dolores asks with her usual wit.

"No. But she has none." They share a look, Spencer's gaze implying that is not normal. "I mean she has none, inside or out. Are you hearing me?" Dolores and Mendez look at each other. Spencer continues, "Anyway, I'm still trying to get to know her better. But she doesn't offer much to talk about."

"Not all people talk a mile a minute. Some people are quiet, reserved." Dolores candidly points out.

"That's just it. She isn't reserved at all. She just never talks about herself. Have you ever met a model who doesn't talk about herself?" Spencer smirks.

"I don't know that many models, really." Mendez says as he picks up a fashion magazine next to him. Xen is on the cover. He stares at her picture for a moment.

With a curt glare, Dolores snatches the magazine away from her husband. "And let's keep it that way." Spencer chuckles as Dolores clears her throat and coolly poses, "The core of consciousness is humility, Spencer. Didn't you say that? Wasn't that the theme of your first movie?"

"I know." Spencer promptly concurs. "I like that about her. She doesn't brag and, she's not self-centered the least bit. But at the same time, I feel she's not telling me something about her job. Like she's hiding something." He looks concerned.

"She goes on photo shoots. What's to tell?" Mendez replies.

"That's just it. I really want the boring chit chat, normal get to know you stuff. She reads all the time, but she doesn't talk about any of that, either. I ask her about the magazine layout, what company, and what not. She just says different magazines, different companies." Spencer continues, "Look, I deal with models and actresses. It's my job. None of the other girls are like this. You can't get a word in sometimes, because most of them are too busy going on and on about who provided the dress they're wearing and who did their hair and yada, yada." He concludes, rolling his eyes.

"What does this have to do with the X files?" Mendez asks.

"Nothing really. I was just curious. I told you. She has strange habits and it's making me think." Spencer gets up to refresh their martinis. "For instance, she always insists on paying for lunch, dinner, whatever. And get this. She only pays in hundreds, like she doesn't know there's different denominations of money."

"Lucky you. I know a lot of people who don't trust banks. People of the ancient traditions view bankers and money lenders as some of the worst kinds of gangsters. They gather together in their secret society to control economies and move forward their dastardly agendas." Dolores is getting tipsy.

Spencer continues. "I've never been to her apartment, never met her family, or any of her friends. She doesn't even talk about them. I know she's from Colorado somewhere, but not a peep other than that."

Dolores stands after receiving a fresh martini. With drink in hand, she leisurely goes to look out the window. She turns to look at them and begins to tell a story.

"Merizo went spear fishing near Cocos Island. With astonishment he spotted a statue of the Virgin Mary on the ocean floor. He swam underwater to try to approach the statue, but to his surprise it retreated. No matter how hard he tried, he couldn't get to the statue."

The guys share a look; *Oh boy, here we go.*

"Merizo returned to shore and sought counsel from the village priest. The priest told the slovenly clad fisherman to dress in his Sunday best and try again. He did so, and this time, Merizo had no trouble getting the statue. You boys are such simpletons." Dolores laughs. "Try a different approach, Spencer. Wear your Sunday best!"

"She was staring up into the sky the other night, in the dark, just staring." Spencer stares at the ceiling as he describes it.

"Oh Spencer." Dolores chuckles. "Are you saying she has some kind of connection to other worlds?"

"Whoa. No, I'm not saying that at all. But what would you do if you were me?" Spencer asks, "Her phone rang in the middle of the night and my lights started flickering." He points at a lamp near him. "I mean, who's calling her at three in the morning, and why am I having electrical shortages all of a sudden? This building is brand new. That just shouldn't happen."

The apartment door suddenly swings open, startling the three of them. It's Xen, with a bag of groceries and some happy birthday mylar balloons. Xen puts the bag of groceries on the kitchen counter.

"Special Agent Horatio Mendez. How the hell are ya?" Xen, beaming, marches up to Mendez and firmly shakes his hand. "And Mrs. Mendez, the Pacific Island Goddess, you are looking lovely as always." Xen leans slightly forward and air-kisses Dolores on both cheeks, a perfect 'faire la bise.'

"Oh, look how beautiful you are, so full of life, joy and positivity." Dolores is delightfully amused to see her.

Xen struts over to Spencer and gives him a passionate full kiss on his unexpecting lips. Dolores and Mendez are watching, smiling, and speechless. Xen looks into Spencer's eyes, then she swiftly turns about. She catwalks like she's working a fashion runway as she puts the groceries away. Spencer recovers.

"Hello Xen. What's new?" Mendez says smoothly, tugging slightly at his shirt collar. He's attempting to return the modish, sexy vibe back to a slightly more, serene tone.

"What's new is I'm making dinner for my new beau here, it being his birthday and all. All organic and natural." Xen says, as she places items from the bag into the refrigerator. "I learned he doesn't like chicken, even though he had chicken leftovers in his fridge the other night." She pauses and looks away for a second, speaking rhetorically, "Who knows why?"

Spencer offers no explanation. He is captivated just watching her talk.

Xen quickly returns her attention to the remaining groceries.

"I got a vegetarian feast planned. I even picked me up a vegetarian cookbook." She drops the book on the counter.

Mendez reaches for the book and notices the sales receipt on the counter next to it. His perceptive self can't help but examine the transaction details: TOTAL $21.57 and CHANGE DUE $79.43. *Elementary, my dear Watson.* He opens the book. "I heard about this one."

"Spencer, did you ask these fine people to come down to the restaurant on Sunday?" Xen locks her provoking blue-green eyes on Spencer's eyes for a second.

It's just enough time for his face to reveal what he's feeling without him saying a single word. She gets her answer and smirks. Spencer, who had plenty to say about his girlfriend a moment ago, has been absent thus far in this conversation. His expression changes from being punch-drunk and love-struck, to anxiety now. "Uh, you said it wasn't going to be a party..."

"Spencer's birthday." Xen interrupts. "He doesn't like birthdays, but it's just close friends, ain't that so hon?"

Spencer has no reply to give her. His eyes say it all, '*deer in the headlights.*'

"So, how was your trip? I hear you just got back from Europe." Dolores says in an attempt to break the palpable awkward silence.

"Oh, it was good. Those Europeans are so into their history and pomp and circumstance, and whatever. You know." She jests with a smirk as she pulls out a couple tall boy Coors beers from the fridge and grabs the TV remote. "Sorry people, do you mind? I want to see how the Rockies are doing real quick." She offers beers to the others, they refuse. Xen cracks open a tall boy brew. The others silently observe.

She walks over to the TV, changes the channel and finds the baseball game is in the top of the fourth inning. The Arizona Diamondbacks are ahead so far, 4-0. "Curt Schilling is looking like the strike-out leader this season, boy I tell ya." She shakes her head, "This is a tough one for my Rockies." She looks back at everyone. "Those Diamondbacks are really good this year, ain't they?"

The three others are standing quietly still, staring. She brings the cold brew up to her glossy lips. Xen chugs the beer. They all look at each other as Xen finishes and crushes the can within the grasp of her hand, followed by a less than ladylike belch. She continues. "My Broncos are two-and-oh. Great start to the season. Shanahan is a good coach."

Suddenly, the sound of a good hit against the bat is heard. Xen swiftly returns her attention to the game in time to see José Ortiz running hard past a ground ball to third base. The Rockies score on a stunning run batted in. "Yeah baby, we score!" Xen walks over to her friends and high-fives the guys. She goes to give ladylike Dolores one. Dolores is diligently holding her martini. The attempt is just, uncoordinated. Xen retracts her high-five. *Too slow.* She swaggers back into the kitchen to make dinner.

"So, you're a Broncos and Rockies fan?" Menendez asks.

"Since forever, Special Agent Mendez." Xen tosses the empty beer can into the recycle bin.

"Oh, the Broncos are from Denver, that's in Colorado, isn't it?" Dolores promptly interposes. They all laugh. Dolores looks slightly confused.

"And none of that special agent stuff, please just call me Mendez." Mendez grabs his things and motions to his wife as they prepare to leave.

"You are staying for dinner, right?" Xen points at them.

"We have reservations." Dolores smiles, taking the last drink of her martini. Her cheeks are rosier than before now.

"Okay. See you Sunday at the Red Onion in Santa Monica for Spencer's party. Six o'clock." Xen glances at Spencer, who becomes slightly anxious, again.

"Yeah. See you there." Mendez says as they leave.

CHAPTER 6
A PECULIAR, BUT EXPECTED, PHONE CALL

A SHORT WHILE LATER, Spencer and Xen are having dinner. There's an unexpected knock at the door. The couple look at each other as Spencer gets up. He walks over to the door and looks into the peep hole, then quietly opens the door. It's a smiling, well-dressed young woman. Spencer steps back without saying a word; a simple silent gesture to invite her in. She is about to speak just as she notices Xen sitting at the dinner table. It is an awkward moment. The woman's lips begin to move, though she seems at a loss for words. She blurts, "Sorry Spencer, I didn't know you had company."

"Who is it?" Xen curiously inquires, already making her way towards the door. Xen promptly stands directly in front of Spencer as she greets their new guest. "And you are?"

"Bella. I'm a friend of Spencer's." Bella nods at Spencer as he leans around Xen. "I just wanted to leave this…"

"So, you're the famous Bella Dia." Xen perks up, smiling. "No, no, no. You are not leaving. It would be terribly rude of me to allow that. Please come in." Xen gestures insistently for Bella to enter.

They quietly gather and sit at the dinner table, as Xen continues, "I've heard all about you. You and Spencer had a tough breakup. So sorry to hear."

Bella, grinning, is slightly taken aback with the unanticipated peculiar remark. "What is the nature of your visit, dear?" Xen asks sterilely, sounding quite like an office assistant at any doctor's office. Then she smiles courteously, as Bella quietly puts a small wrapped giftbox she had been holding on the table. But before Bella opens her mouth to reply, Xen suddenly reacts to a play from the baseball game on the TV. "Yes! Run Ortiz! Dammit, run man, run!"

There was a solid, line drive hit from Jeff Cirillo of the Rockies to center field. Jose Ortiz comes to a sliding halt at third base as Juan Pierre scores. "Yes!" Xen exclaims, as she high-fives Spencer. Next, she reaches towards Bella sitting across the table for a quick, air-high-five. Bella awkwardly reacts off cadence. Xen retracts her high-five. *Too slow.*

"Nice swing." Spencer remarks, nodding encouragingly at Bella. He is slightly flustered. Bella gives a courtesy smile and chuckles. She is slightly flustered, as well.

"Awe man!" Xen sulks aloud, startling Bella and Spencer. The top of the sixth inning is now suddenly over after a groundball force-out to second base. "That Curt Schilling is just killing us!" Xen looks at Bella and Spencer. She giggles at her own humor, "Hey, that rhymes. I made a rhyme."

Spencer responds with a nod and a smile. He doesn't know how else to reply to that. All the same, Bella offers another courtesy chuckle.

Xen says to Bella, sweetly, "Stay. Have dinner with us."

"I couldn't..."

"Nonsense." Xen interrupts Bella, "It'll be fab. Right Spencer?" Spencer acknowledges with a slight grin and a shrug of his shoulders. Xen turns to Bella, "So what's on your mind?"

"Well, Spencer's birthday. I was just stopping by to wish him a happy birthday and give him his gift. I know he wouldn't have a party." Bella looks directly at Xen and says sincerely, "But things are over with us. We're just friends."

"Oh, I know that Bella." Xen replies with a consoling tone of voice. "He told me all about it. I'm not jealous. Jealousy is a sign of the ego run amok. My ego is in check, so I never get stuck in a muck." Xen, chuckles at her latest rhyme improv.

Spencer acknowledges with a reflective pout and, a nod. Bella just stares onward in perplexity of it all.

"Come. Let's break bread, get to know one another. You don't mind Spencer, do you?" Xen, beaming, turns to Spencer.

He raises a brow and nods in consent. Xen proceeds to serve Bella a full plate of food. They eat. There is more awkward silence. Then, Xen's mobile phone suddenly rings.

The kitchen and dining area lights flicker at that exact moment. Bella looks around, baffled by the peculiar coincidence. Spencer stares at Bella. He knows she notices the lights.

Xen immediately sees No Caller ID displayed on her cell phone. "I better take this." She answers the call.

Xen stands as she starts speaking to the caller. "I know it's you who's been blowing up my phone and hanging up. Who are you? How did you get my number? It doesn't matter. Listen, pervert! You better stop calling me and you better not come near me. I know Karate and Jujitsu. If you come close to me, I'll be teaching you some lessons." Bella and Spencer are quiet. Spencer is impressed. Xen never mentioned about her martial arts skills.

"You have something that belongs to friends of mine." Xen hears the solemn voice of a man.

She replies at once, with a relaxed deferential tone of voice. "Oh, yes. My mistake sir. Yes sir, yes sir. Hold on a minute."

Bella and Spencer look at each other as Xen opens the apartment door. She steps into the hallway and gently closes the door behind her.

"We knew you would research us. We have been trying to call you, to give you your instructions." The line is silent. "Are you okay Xen?"

Xen is impressed. The mysterious gentleman called her by her nickname. "Yes. I'm okay. How do you know me? Why me? How do you know I can be trusted? How do I know I can trust you? I have so many questions."

Xen has been wondering about this moment. She anticipated that this would soon happen. She is not surprised to receive this peculiar phone call. She remembered what she had read regarding the significance of the gems and, what they must mean to the trusted peoples that keep them. Xen had theorized, someone special and appointed probably would try to get the mysterious diamonds back. She listens anxiously for his reply.

"We've been watching you, well my friends have."

Hearing that, Xen tests her theory. She wants to be certain this is not a perverted, prank caller. "This all sounds like a sincere invasion of privacy to me." Xen looks around the hallway, patiently awaiting what the response would be to her challenging conjecture.

"It's not like that." The man's voice is calm and assured. "My friends don't spy. They just accumulate data, observe from a distance and, deduce from there."

"No one's been following me. I've been trained to detect any tail and shake it just as fast." Xen snaps her fingers in nonchalant reply.

"My friends have surveillance technology that your instincts wouldn't detect." His response is sincere and candid. "My friends mean you no harm. If they were going to harm you, they would have done so already."

"I'm not afraid." Her response is exacting, confident.

"When I speak in transcendental, fourth dimensional terms I am speaking metaphorically. Can you accept that?" The mysterious man calmly continues to explain. "My friends know you are one of a small number of fully conscious and present people on this planet. Other people see your ever-present state of mind as quirky and funny. Fortunately, you are easy on the eyes, so you don't get as much criticism as others. But you must use your extraordinary combination of abilities and characteristics to stimulate your innate persuasive skills, to bring more people into consciousness. Once the number of fully conscious people reaches a large enough level, we can share more information, and you will learn more. In the meantime, you must trust."

"I am beginning to trust you." Xen replies.

"You have studied the calm of the martial arts masters. We knew you wouldn't panic. The nature of your business has taught you discretion. We knew you would keep things to yourself and seek knowledge."

"What happened that caused the stones to be removed from their usual place?" Her curiosity stirs. Xen is certain these are the keepers of the precious Almasi Ya Kifo diamonds.

"That is not a topic for this conversation."

"If your friends are so powerful, why don't they just figure out some high-tech way to get the diamonds back?"

"Well, two reasons. The more of their technology they utilize the more attention they bring to themselves. Second, recruiting enlightened people brings them to our tribe, thus we spread enlightenment, presence, positivity. These are values of supreme importance to my friends and, to my people."

"It's hard to believe that a native tribe possesses this level of tech. You are from a native tribe?" Xen politely inquires, although she has a good idea by now.

His response is fluid. "Yes, the Paiutes. You can say I am the brain trust for all... interested parties." He continues, "But the Paiutes are not the possessors of the technology. We are the keepers of the diamonds. We are trusted for our profound spiritual connection, reverence for tradition, respect of nature. My friends trust us, as they now have come to learn about and trust you. The tribes you have been studying, the Xhosa in South Africa, the Gunggari, Aboriginal and Pacific Straight Islanders in Australia, the Paiute, and the others have never used spiritual teachings for material gain."

Xen listens intently. She appreciates having this opportunity to learn more about the mysterious diamonds. She hears the sincere and compelling tone in his voice. She wonders how soon they will meet. *Who are these people?*

He continues, "The human race is at a crossroads. As technology advances humankind can be swept into consciousness, goodness, peace. Or it can be forced into divisiveness, fearmongering and panic. It all depends on the possessors of new technologies and how they are applied."

"The books don't really tell me why the Almasi Ya Kifo diamonds are so dangerous, though they are very rare and valuable?" Xen replies in consideration of the facts she read.

"These stones have a certain energy. All matter has specific energy. Man learns to harness that energy and make machinery, computers, aircraft and so on. These stones have an energy that acts as a power supply. But they also have other qualities. They vibrate the energy of the possessor and can directly focus an intensity to produce an outcome. Whether it be a desirable or undesirable one. Yet, this concept is not unfamiliar. Consider the healing powers of holistic stones, for example. Those exist. The diamonds in your possession retain those qualities on a much higher scale, to an extent many would not believe to be possible." His assertion is calm and earnest. "The stones in your keep at present. They have a capacity that can allow you the ability to essentially, walk-through walls."

"I've never heard of anything like that." Xen is rapt.

"Humankind is not ready to know, yet."

"You keep referring to your friends. I want to meet them."

"You are not ready for that, either." His response is more guarded now. "You have two choices. You can trust and follow my instructions."

"Or?" Xen replies promptly, very curious of her options.

"Sell the diamonds to the highest bidder." He proposes matter of fact, "If you do, you will be a wealthy woman. You will never have to work another day of your life. If that is your choice, we will not bother you again."

Xen still hasn't opened the jewelry box. She has no interest or desire to look upon the diamonds and ogle at their lustrous worth. And she hasn't once considered the option of selling them for egocentric profit. That just didn't feel right to her. She still feels the tranquil, contentment holding onto the gems. That same reassuring feeling, deep inside, remains. More so, Xen has the greatest satisfaction having the opportunity now to return the mysterious diamonds to their rightful owner.

"Money is not that important to me. But you already knew that." She says, acknowledging that they must.

"Twenty-one thirty hours, Sunday. Bring the diamonds." His reply is candid. "Lake Arrowhead. You already know the coordinates. Tell no one. Come alone." He pauses for a slight moment, "Also, one more thing. Be easy on Spencer. Your shared beliefs regarding human nature, your value systems, drew you together. He was not born with your instincts. He has spent his whole life learning and advocating, but he is not quite there yet. Give him time. Be patient."

"Whoa!" Xen perks up, "Now wait just one second there, dearie. That is way too personal." The phone line has gone silent, dead. Xen doesn't notice and, she continues to ramble. "How do you know who Spencer is? Have you been following him, too? Is he in danger? Should I be worried? Because he doesn't know how to detect being followed like I can." She goes on, talking about her boyfriend. "So, you guys like him, too. I think he's a very special guy. What do your friends think?" Xen looks at her phone, realizing now she is talking to no one.

Just then, Spencer opens the door and looks at her, concerned.

"You okay, Xen?" Spencer leans out the door to look down the hallway. "Everything okay?"

Xen smiles at him. "I'm fine." She walks towards the door, and she hugs him. They go back inside.

CHAPTER 7
MR. ANGELINO

I T IS A beautiful Sunday morning along a picturesque mountain road overlooking what is largely, San Bernardino County. A tall, fit 45-year-old man with long blonde hair and dressed in Harley gear is taking a break. He is relaxing, sitting next to his new motorcycle, a 2001, Dyna Wide Glide Harley-Davidson. He has dark Spy sunglasses on, gazing at the valley below. The view from the scenic stop he just parked at is spectacular. He is taking this peaceful moment to read an important letter that is personally addressed to him. It reads:

Dear Mr. Angelino,

Your parole officer has said that your prison stay has left you contemplating your actions and you have taken the time to learn and grow. Take advantage of this first delivery and it could turn into a full-time job that pays well and will provide for your family. We only ask that you do not reveal the details of these deliveries including address, senders or receivers or any other details. Your pickup and delivery instructions are attached in a separate letter.

Best of success.
Mr. Jones, Manager
REDEMPTION DELIVERY SERVICES
Compton, CA

CHAPTER 8
OTHER-WORLDLY LIFE EXISTS

Later that Sunday at the Red Onion in Santa Monica, Spencer's closest friends have come to celebrate his birthday. They are socializing in a reserved dining area for the private occasion. There are appetizers, drinks and a large birthday cake surrounded by some mylar balloons on an outdoor patio table. Xen is working the room, charming everyone she meets. Bella and Spencer are sitting, casually chatting. They are observing Xen, who turns around, smiles brightly, and gives them a thumbs-up. Then, Xen resumes talking to everyone near her.

"Maybe she's not like some of your other girlfriends who had issues with us being friends. She's just not the jealous type like they were." Bella supposes while observing Xen.

"I understand about someone not being the jealous type, but this is ridiculous." Spencer replies in a low tone of voice, gesturing as he speaks, "You and I've been on again, off again since we were kids. For all she knows you and I could rekindle and then so much for her and me."

"You think she doesn't care?" Bella answers, leaning forward and making direct eye contact with him to make her point.

"That's just it. She does. I know she does. I'm sure of it." Spencer replies sincerely.

"Aren't you the one who preaches about the futility of jealousy?

How it drives the other person away? How we need to check our egos?"

"Yeah, but we're all human right? We all feel jealous some of the time. Right?" Spencer says shaking his head, "It's like, the way she thinks and acts, it's not human sometimes."

"Are you saying she's some kind of alien from outer space? Or maybe she's an android?" Bella retorts, chuckling.

"No, no, no, course not." He replies just as Xen waves and smiles at him. He smiles and waves back.

"What are you saying, Spencer?" Bella frowns disapprovingly. "Sounds like you're fumbling for a reason NOT to like her. Are you getting tired of her, already? Huh?"

"No, no, no, course not!" Then, Spencer lowers his tone again as he tries to explain. "That phone call." He declares, raising his hand, as if he wants a judge to submit evidence in a court trial. "You know. Remember? The lights started to flicker like they usually do when she gets a call. And she wouldn't tell me who she was talking to."

"Maybe, it was just a coincidence, or something is wrong with your electrics, whatever it is." Bella shrugs, "I don't know, there's probably an explanation. And the phone call is none of my business, or yours, Spencer." Bella glares.

"She doesn't drive." Spencer has more to say. "She doesn't even have a license. She doesn't have a car, and she has money. She walks, rides her bike, takes taxis. Who takes taxis in LA? Freakin' taxis!" Spencer is keeping his voice lowered as best he can.

Xen winks at Spencer from across the dining area. Spencer smiles and nods.

Bella sighs heavily, becoming more perturbed. "Maybe she's out to protect the environment. She's part hippie. Spencer, who cares really? Anyway, I gotta go. I have an early start and a long drive tomorrow. I'm leaving. I don't even know why I came." Bella shakes her head and rolls her eyes. She stands up abruptly and walks over to where

Xen is socializing. Spencer watches Bella casually saying her goodbyes to others.

Brock walks over to Spencer. They watch Xen and Bella hug. "What is your ex-girlfriend doing here?" Brock asks amusingly, while gently swirling his gin and tonic on the rocks in hand.

"Xen invited her." Spencer replies as Bella begins to walk intently towards Brock and Spencer.

As Bella passes directly in-between Spencer and Brock, she butts her shoulder into Spencer. She doesn't say a word, and she doesn't slow down. They both turn to watch Bella walk out of the private dining area. She doesn't look back.

Brock leans closer to Spencer, saying just above a whisper, "You're popular."

"Shut up." Spencer coolly responds. Then he asks his buddy, "What did you find out about her? Anything else?"

"Everyone in the business loves her. She graduated from U.C. Boulder, language studies. Came out to LA right after and started modelling. She reads, plays beach volleyball, volunteers at the soup kitchen, she's nice to stray animals. Nothing you don't already know." Brock takes a sip of his cocktail.

"Look at her." Spencer nods. They look at Xen who is speaking with an older gentleman. Xen blows Spencer a kiss. "She never gets tired. She never complains. She's never scared. It's not natural."

Brock chuckles, "Spencer, chillax! Who's the one who rants on and on about the uselessness of complaining, and what most humans fear, is an illusion? Sound familiar? It should. You freakin' wrote a whole damn book about it." Brock puts a hand on his buddy's shoulder. "Your super-hot fashion model girlfriend is living what you preach, and you freak out. Doctor, heal thyself." Brock shakes his head, chuckling.

"Yes. But it's too much though, can't you see it?" Spencer says as

Xen finds Mendez and Dolores eating hors d'oeuvres and gives the couple an exaggerated thumbs-up.

"You're saying she's some kind of a bionic woman or something?" Brock smirks.

"No, I'm not saying that. But what if she was? Or what if she had some kind of connection to technology that we don't know of, or understand?" Spencer is serious.

"Now that's crazy talk." Brock grimaces. "Don't screw this up, Spencer. Just enjoy her man. Come on. Take a chill pill." Brock motions for Spencer to walk with him back to the group.

They both walk outside onto the dining patio. There is a small gathering of people there standing around Dr. Alistair Hammershtat. He is an eccentric 60-year-old, African American, wearing a traditional three-piece suit and glasses. He is a very distinguished professor. Xen approaches him. She has a tall glass in her hand, the contents being only premium round ice cubes.

Xen says excitedly, "Doctor Alistair Hammershtat. I'm so glad you accepted my invitation."

Spencer, head cocked to one side, looks at him. *Who is he?*

Xen notices Spencer and pulls her boyfriend close to her, whispering, "Doctor Hammershtat is an expert on quantum physics and extraterrestrial sightings and such. I've attended many of his lectures and read his books. I thought he'd be a great conversation starter here at your party."

Spencer, head still tilted, stares wide-eyed at Xen.

Dr. Hammershtat begins to speak. "Machu Picchu, Mexico City pyramids, and Egyptian pyramids, are small samples of proof that other-worldly life exists. But what form of life?" He peers at everyone near him.

Xen looks up into the evening sky. Dr. Hammershtat looks up as well. She tosses one of the round ice cubes from her glass into her mouth and begins to chomp on it like a machine. Spencer stares in astonishment.

The professor continues. "But not like science fiction movies, universes populated with humanoids and androids and bizarre creatures. Whenever we are visited by extraterrestrial life, they are like a zookeeper walking into the chimpanzee paddock. They look around, take some pictures, then leave without interacting significantly with the environment. Meanwhile the busy chimps have no idea what just happened."

Xen is listening intently, almost hypnotized. Mendez and Dolores have been observing the conversation. They make eye contact with Spencer. *Who is he?* Spencer shrugs his shoulders discretely.

"And what if their intentions are sketchy?" Xen inquires, still chewing on her ice.

"Even if they reveal themselves as the worst kinds of deviants, sexually obsessed, nasty smelling, and painful to look at. They're here, I want to know about them, study them, include them. Scold them, praise them." The professor boldly affirms.

Xen, like the professor and the others standing near them, are enthralled looking towards the early evening sky. No one says another word.

Brock breaks the silence. "Dr. Hammershtat, tell me more."

Meanwhile, Spencer, Mendez and Dolores have quietly slipped away from the small group standing in the patio. They watch Xen from the indoor lounge. She is still busy socializing with everyone. A server approaches the three of them with a tray of cocktails. Spencer, Mendez and Dolores retrieve their drinks and thank the server. Dolores starts to giggle, watching Xen interact with the socialite guests.

"Such a darling of a girlfriend you have there, Spencer. She's so polite to everyone. She's everybody's BFF." Dolores is a little tipsy.

"That Area Fifty-One and X-File subdivision intel sure is touchy.

No one talks about it." Mendez affirms, "She's not on any list that I know of."

"She bats her eyes at the night sky." Spencer says, staring into his fresh martini.

"You're nuts. Like she's trying to communicate with the mother ship?" Dolores laughs.

Just then, Xen taps lightly on the patio window outside and waves at them, then turns back around to continue talking to the guests. Spencer, Mendez and Dolores sit quietly and continue to enjoy their cocktails.

Xen suddenly enters the lounge area. "Come on hon, have some cake." She takes Spencer by the arm and leads him back outside to the patio. Mendez and Dolores follow.

"I'll cut the cake." Dolores offers politely. She goes to grab the knife. It slips in her soft grip and she cuts her finger.

Xen hurries over and immediately starts emptying her oversized purse. She pulls out numerous items, including the TRIBALISM OF SOUTH AFRICA AND NATIVE AMERICA book, and the airline ticket stub for the recent trip to Italy. She places the items on top of the patio table. Spencer notices the airline ticket stub. Unnoticed by anyone, Xen's notebook also falls from her purse onto the floor. Xen finally pulls out a band aid and helps Dolores.

As Xen starts putting things back in her purse, Spencer suddenly tells her what he's thinking. "You told me you were going to Germany. The ticket says Italy. If you were going to Italy why not just say so?"

Xen looks at him, confused.

"Who keeps calling you in the middle of the night?" He persists, "I'm not jealous. I just wanna know."

Mendez and Dolores share a look, suddenly becoming uncomfortable. Dolores excuses herself and heads to the lady's room. Mendez steps back to allow the couple a little more privacy. Mendez has his drink to keep him occupied now.

"Not that it's any of your business but I did go to Germany." Xen frowns saying, "I also went to Italy. I never lied to you. Spencer, I'm a private person. You don't know me well enough for me to share it all. You gotta earn that. You're so into your books and your movies and your seminars and speeches. And I'm your biggest fan. But you haven't shown any more than mild interest in me, a curious interest. Once I see more from you, I will open up, maybe. But at this point, I have to give serious consideration if we should even continue." She shakes her head, frowning. "Know what? I'm gonna leave now."

"Wait, because of this? Come on, no." Spencer immediately replies, softly pleading. "Come on, Xen."

"I was really starting to like you, Spencer."

"At least let me drive you home." Spencer appeals.

"No." Xen looks away and raises her hand, dismissing him. Xen grabs the rest of her things, as Spencer continues to softly plead. She walks away from him, making her way through all the guests, and saying goodbye to them. Spencer watches, standing in the same spot where she left him. Before long, she's walking towards the main exit. Xen walks off, not looking back at Spencer. But she leaves the notebook behind. No one notices.

As she leaves, Brock walks up. He leans in close to Spencer. "Ouch!" Brock quips, "Talk to the hand, eh? Do you ever listen to anyone? I told you not to screw things up. So, you go and do the exact opposite. Good job!" Brock says mockingly, as he pats Spencer on the shoulder and winks.

Spencer is shaken. He doesn't look at Brock. He is too ashamed to reply.

Then, Mendez notices the notebook on the floor. "Hey, who's notebook? Maybe Xen dropped it?" Mendez steps closer, picks it up, and hands it over to Spencer.

"Xen must have dropped it." Spencer answers, as he opens it. He looks quickly through it. There are some hand-written notes along with several drawings of a Native American ceremony. There is a peculiar drawing of what appears to be a jewel, emitting shining light. There are also written longitude and latitude coordinates. "What the hell is all this shit?" Spencer looks at his friends. "The Paiute Tribe?"

"Did you say Paiute?" Mendez looks closer at the notebook. "They were mentioned in the X files documents."

Spencer silently reads through a few of the notes. Then he says with a puzzled look, "Almasi Ya Kifo?"

"What did you say?!" Brock responds, pulling the notebook closer to have a look. His face is showing legitimate terror. "Let me see that. Almasi Ya Kifo! Bro, it's a diamond, but next level shit! The African legend, the tribal people, they say they're cursed, the Almasi diamonds. They're used in some voodoo rituals and what not. You touch them and turn to stone and shit like that." Brock snaps his finger. "Serious deadly bling!"

"Bro, you don't believe that bullshit, do you?" Spencer smirks, looking at Mendez for support. Mendez ponders, with raised brow and pursed lips. *It could be true?*

"I don't know." Brock replies, "But I do know they are very valuable. One small stone the size of a kid's marble could fetch six, maybe seven figures, easy. People kill for those diamonds. If Xen is mixed up in them and those voodoo tribes, man. It's not safe." He shakes his head, deadpan serious.

"Let me see those coordinates." Mendez looks carefully at some of the writing in the notebook again. "The one that's circled, that's Lake Arrowhead."

There is a scribble in the notebook indicating a place and time to meet: Next to the bridge near the lake. 9:30 PM Sunday. Tonight.

Spencer looks at his watch and says, "I'm going."

"Call me. I can meet you up there with a couple of my guys. Let me know if you need me, Spencer." Mendez nods.

"Thanks Mendez. I'll let you know if I do." Spencer replies as he turns to leave.

Mendez wishes him well. Brock is concerned. Dolores returns just in time to watch Spencer walk away. The other guests continue socializing and making new friends. Slightly, just above the other conversations within the quaint gathering, Dr. Hammershtat is clearly heard questioning rhetorically, "I wonder, are we still having cake?"

CHAPTER 9
WEIRD SCIENCE

NOT FAR FROM the bridge where Xen is soon destined to be, Heather is at her favorite local ice cream parlor. Heather is a cheery, 18-year-old high school senior, who looks much younger for her age. She is waiting with anticipatory pleasure to place her order. She knows exactly what she wants. Finally, the server is ready for her order.

"I'll have a peanut butter and jelly, chunky monkey and salted caramel, three scoops!" Heather beams, wide-eyed, speaking up clearly to make sure he gets it right.

Heather has been waiting for this moment all week. She worked hard during cheerleading practice. She volunteered an extra shift at the soup kitchen last Tuesday. She was really busy with her church youth outreach program yesterday. Not to mention she also completed a few of her school semester assignments early last week, including a nomadic peoples history project. She needed some ice cream tonight, after all that. She had earned it. Fittingly, Heather does a silent enthusiastic clap of glee when she is handed her ultimate reward for all her challenging work.

Heather pays for her deserved indulgence with some of the generous allowance that her father gives her. He gave her extra cash this time, because of her recent accomplishments over the past several weeks. Her father insists she doesn't work right now, like some of her high school friends do. He prefers she volunteer her time and learn how to really be of great benefit to people. *"Give your time and effort willingly for the benefit of others in need. Blessings will follow,"* says her *father.*

· · · • • ● • • · ·

XEN HAS ARRIVED at the designated meeting point. She has a small backpack that is tightly fastened. Hidden inside are the treasured, Almasi Ya Kifo diamonds. She has not taken the jewelry case out to look at its beguiling contents, confirming she has them. She doesn't need to check and see if they are still inside the case. She feels the presence of the stones. It is a feeling like knowing someone kind is standing right next to you. It's that warm reassuring feeling Xen is becoming more aware of, each day. She feels unexplainably peaceful when she is near the jewels.

Xen looks at her backpack, wondering how the keepers feel when the diamonds are near them. She wonders if they feel the same, calm and reassuring emotion she is experiencing right now. She is unaware of the greediness that can suddenly intensify and utterly engulf a person that pursues the stones for voracious profit. She doesn't know greed causes an intensification of a particular vibration of circum-stance that brings serious detriment, sometimes very quickly. In other words, more greed channels more adversity, towards the greed.

Xen is admiring the view of the lake mountain town situated just across the bridge. She enjoys the view of all the lights. It's busy tonight. Most of the tourists visiting the Lake Arrowhead shopping area have come from the lower valley. Xen is standing near the popular, scenic lakeside drive. The road winds around the large lake, eventually leading into the main intersection of the town. She can faintly hear the lively traffic of tourists and automobiles across the way, in the peaceful, still of the evening. Xen looks up towards the vast heavens. Something she frequently enjoys doing. The evening sky is so lovely, full of shiny, wondrous stars.

At that moment, Spencer approaches slowly from the side. In the near distance there are two other figures lurking in the darkness, unnoticed.

Xen hears something. She looks to her left, and notices Spencer. "Spencer, what the hell are you doing here?!" She challenges in a heavy whisper.

Spencer shows her the notebook. "You left it at the restaurant. I wasn't snooping. But we did look at it and we were all concerned. Mendez knew about the Paiutes and Brock told me about the Almasi... whatever they are. I thought you could be in danger." Spencer is sincere, and Xen hears the genuine concern in his tone of voice.

"I can take care of myself, Spencer." She snatches the notebook from Spencer. *You're not getting off that easy, hon!*

"I'm sorry about giving you the third degree. I have no right." Spencer looks ashamed, and sincerely regretful.

"Dammed right you don't!"

"Look, I really am into you, more than you know, Xen. It's not just because you're a model and pretty and popular and all. You're calm, cool, collected and, that magic kiss. Whoa! It's like, if I could create you, this would be the creation, like in Weird Science or something." Spencer chuckles.

"Weird Science?" Xen manages to crack a smile. "So, you think I'm a lab creation, or some kind of robot or something?" She tilts her head playfully like a robot, and they both laugh.

"You are kind of strange, ya gotta admit." They laugh together. "Look, I never really shared how I felt. I was playing aloof, being confident, you know, so you'd think I'm cool." Spencer shrugs, smirks.

"Spencer. I brag about you all the time, what a great speaker and storyteller you are. How you weave those stories and lessons into motivational movies. You know that?" Xen says as they step closer to one another, "I already see you as the cool guy. Just be yourself. Be real, hon."

"I will." Spencer gently pulls her close. They kiss.

Xen says while he holds her close, "Aside from modelling, I'm into some other jobs, other important projects, which are, let's just say, confidential. I can't tell you, not yet. Can you accept that?"

"Yes." Spencer respectfully acknowledges. The two mysterious strangers begin to walk closer now, still unnoticed. Spencer says, "I don't mean to pry and tell me if I'm being nosy, but what the hell are you doing all the way out here?" They both laugh together.

"For some strange reason, I came into possession of the Almasi Ya Kifo diamonds. I can't really go into detail about how, except to say, it was part of my modeling job." Xen divulges only a little information.

Spencer interrupts, "Brock freaked out about those. Said none of the diamond people mess with them."

"Yeah. I sort of heard the same thing. Somehow and, for reasons I'm still figuring out, they were entrusted to me for safekeeping." Xen shakes her head, listening to her own astonishing explanation as she speaks, "I need to get them back to their rightful owners and this is where I needed to bring them. I knew it could be dangerous, but they trust me. And I trust them. I have to."

· · · · • ● • · ·

AFTER ENJOYING A relaxing day spending time and riding around nearby Big Bear Lake, Mr. Angelino was ready to start his first job assignment. He headed towards Lake Arrowhead, so he could arrive for his pickup time with time to spare. He was following the specific instructions of the letter addressed to him very carefully. Now, Mr. Angelino is gliding along a dark windy road, fast approaching the same location where Xen and Spencer happen to be.

. . . . ● ● ● . . .

By this time, Heather has made her way walking to get to her favorite spot. She lives nearby. She often rides her bike along this same path. But this evening, she wanted to enjoy the ice cream and walk. Heather is at the bridge where she likes to look at the lights of the town by the lake. She is close to where Xen and Spencer are standing right now.

. . . ● ● ● . . .

The mysterious figures lurking in the dark approach the couple. Spencer notices them first. He is startled. Xen is not. They see a tall Native American man in his forties, dressed in a handsome business suit and bolo tie. The other person is a woman. She is taller. She is dressed in a snug, long sleeve Habesha kemis style dress, with matching niqab style head dress and gloves. She is covered from head to toe. Only her eyes show.

"Xenyatta Davenport. We knew you would come. I am Chief Amitola. This is Shurze." The man says, "You have something that belongs to my friends."

Xen nods, as she slowly takes the case containing the Almasi Ya Kifo diamonds out of her backpack. She hands the case to Chief Amitola, asking, "Will we meet again?"

"It is possible." Chief Amitola replies candidly. Next, he and his companion Shurze turn around and quietly walk away together. They return to the dark corner of the road where they came from, practically disappearing into the night.

"Holy shit! That was legit!" Spencer responds in a heavy, low tone of voice. He has an arm around Xen, holding her close.

"Yeah, it was." Xen turns to him. They hug and share a passionate kiss.

· · · • • ● • • · · ·

From out of the dark side of the other corner behind Spencer and Xen, Heather is coming. Her ice cream treat is almost finished. She strolls along quietly, looking at the lovely view of the town across the lake. Heather gets almost halfway across the small bridge when she decides to cross the quiet narrow road. She takes one look for traffic. She waits for a car to pass by that she sees. Without taking another look Heather steps off the curb, still enjoying the remaining portion of her ice cream cone.

At that exact moment, Mr. Angelino is approaching the bridge, very quickly. Heather saw the previous car when she first looked, but she did not notice the Harley-Davidson close behind it. She heard the noises of other automobiles on the adjacent main road nearby, but she did not realize the motorcycle was rapidly closing the distance.

Mr. Angelino sees Heather look his way, but he didn't know she only noticed the car in front of him. Suddenly, Mr. Angelino swerves, narrowly avoiding a bag with an empty beer can in it. He is looking down, ready to swerve again in case there is more trash. Heather, consumed by the last bite of her ice cream cone, walks into the middle of the road. When Mr. Angelino looks forward again, he is surprised to see the young lady walking directly ahead of him in the middle of the road. There is a look of sheer terror on his face. The motorcycle is sure to hit her.

Chief Amitola and Shurze quietly watch what has transpired. But there is no exclamation of a warning from the two. They say nothing. The only reaction is from Shurze. She quickly places her gloved left hand over the case that Chief Amitola is still carefully holding onto. She opens the case containing the Almasi Ya Kifo diamonds. Suddenly, a blinding white strobe of light emits from the jewels that seemingly takes over the night. Simultaneously, the motorcycle appears to go right through the girl. Shurze methodically closes the case.

What appears to be impossible has just happened. Heather and Mr. Angelino are both, unharmed. Heather looks down, realizing now how close she is to the curb. She carefully steps onto the sidewalk. She's on her way back home. She is unaware of what just happened. The brakes on the motorcycle are just about to lock-up, when Mr. Angelino suddenly realizes, nothing is there. He blinks and, the girl is suddenly, out of the way. He glances to his right and sees she is stepping onto the sidewalk. He shakes it off.

· · · · ● ● ● ● · · ·

Xen and Spencer release their loving kiss, while still embracing. In their intimate caressing moment having their eyes closed, they witnessed nothing. Xen looks directly into Spencer's eyes. "Did you feel that?" Xen utters, sensing something very peculiar has just happened.

"Magic kiss." Spencer smiles, hugging her tenderly, nose to nose. She smiles back. *Curious, just a feeling perhaps,* Xen turns her shoulder and looks down the road.

· · · · ● ● ● ● · · ·

Reformed convict, Mr. Angelino arrives at the delivery location as precisely instructed. He brings his Harley-Davidson to a stop at the dark corner of the road, right in front of Shurze and Chief Amitola. Next, Mr. Angelino opens the leather saddlebag on the side of his motorbike. Chief Amitola methodically places the case containing the mysterious, ethereal diamonds, and a manila envelope inside. Expressionless, without a word said, Mr. Angelino nods to Chief Amitola and Shurze. Then, Mr. Angelino rides off.

Xen and Spencer observe the handoff. They shake their heads, both wondering where the diamonds are headed next. They turn hand in hand, and slowly walk away.

What they don't see is a figure watching them from the shadows.

ACKNOWLEDGMENTS

To our publishing consultant, editor and executive film producer, the incomparable Barbara Lynn. Our motion picture came to be, because of your dedicated hard work and attention to every exacting detail. Not an easy task producing a film during a historic pandemic! And thank you for all you do publishing our creative work. You are a genie in a bottle!

To our talented cast and crew. Our film is an award-winning film, because of all the blessings your skills have brought to our heartfelt production. Cheers to you all!

To our director. The real-deal dirt merchant, Henning Morales. Having the wherewithal to recognize an opportunity bringing together fiction and non-fiction is what helped to make this story remarkable and outspokenly unique.

The blessing of the Lord makes one rich,

And He adds no sorrow with it.

– Proverbs 10:22

New King James Version

THE FATE DIAMOND SERIES
BOOK 1

ALMASI YA KIFO

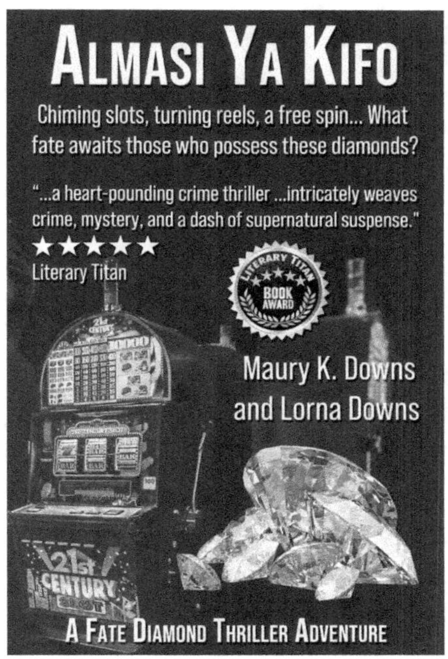

The Almasi Ya Kifo diamonds, respected, esteemed and celebrated by many... feared and cursed by others. Paulo Pineda is a popular and likeable, but somewhat hesitant, young man incessantly seeking quick fortune. Joseph Ashe has more enemies than he has friends. He is not a popular, likeable person, with a criminal record going way back. He recently came into possession of the mysterious Almasi Ya Kifo diamonds, having stolen them from his shady business partner. Quite unexpectantly, Paulo's and Joseph's paths collide, with dramatic affect. Now in possession of the diamonds, Paulo's life turns into a roller coaster adventure... both exhilarating and terrifying.

COMING SOON
THE FATE DIAMOND SERIES
BOOK 3
BARRACUDA

Paulo Pineda is consumed by an unquenchable wanting. He was previously in possession of the Almasi Ya Kifo diamonds. He gave them up out of fear for his life. Now his thoughts are preoccupied with the selfish hope of finding the diamonds and keeping them for himself. Having reluctantly let go of the mysterious diamonds, Paulo persistently dwells on how his luck would be different if he still had them. Then, quite unexpectantly, and by what seems more than coincidence, Paulo encounters the transporter, Xen. Obsessed with possessing the diamonds, Paulo follows Xen.

He's determined, greedy and ruthless in his hunt.
Just like a... Barracuda.

Turn the page to read an excerpt from Barracuda.

CHAPTER 1
I WONDER WHERE MY LUCKY DIAMONDS ARE RIGHT NOW?

Saturday, September 29, 2001

IT'S A TYPICAL hot and sunny afternoon outside on the Las Vegas Strip. Though, Paulo Pineda is quite comfortable. Paulo is sitting inside the plush and colorful Tropicana Las Vegas lobby. The air conditioning inside the huge resort is ideal, nice and cool. He reads the Las Vegas Sun newspaper while patiently waiting for his club deluxe room to be ready.

Paulo is the type of young man incessantly seeking quick fortune. He is an avid gambler who frequents casinos, such as here in Las Vegas more often than he probably should. He is particularly enthusiastic about joining any multilevel marketing gimmick, no matter how risky the scheme may seem. Although a bit withdrawn, he is hasty to seize an opportunity if he thinks it is profitable for him, sometimes to the point of ignorant irresponsibility.

It's crowded. All around him are vacationers and tourists, talking aloud and meandering about. In the near distance, he hears the melodic jingles of slot machines, calling him like a Siren. However, Paulo ignores the beckoning songs of the wagering machines, for now. *There will be plenty of time for that later.* What Paulo needs right now, is a nice long nap. He has had a hectic, eventful Saturday.

· · · · ● · · · ·

Paulo was busy earlier today at Los Angeles International Airport carrying out a meticulous plan his aunt Elvie had cleverly devised. Elvie trades diamonds and other precious gemstones around the world. She is considered an expert by many of her industry associates. As part of her business, she has trusted people that help her secretly get expensive valuables in and out of the country. Today's plan had involved Paulo stashing his precious Almasi Ya Kifo diamonds inconspicuously along with a coincident jewelry transporting job that was taking place.

Paulo had agreed for Elvie to help him get rid of the Almasi Ya Kifo diamonds. Why? So that Paulo could rid himself of the stone's legendary curse. When he had unexpectantly come into possession of the diamonds, he had experienced very strange and disturbing happenings.

Elvie's plan had all transpired without a hitch, almost. Unfortunately, while hastily trying to execute the plan, Paulo had accidentally smacked right into the beautiful transporter. The impact was solid enough to stir up a few gasps from some of the people sitting there at the departure gate. The young lady had fallen to the floor. Her purse, cell phone, and other belongings all strewn about on the floor.

The transporter knocked to the floor just happened to be Xenyatta Davenport, a successful fashion model with a secret freelance side profession. Xenyatta, Xen as her friends know her, was covertly carrying some priceless diamonds for a private insurance company.

Luckily, Paulo had been able to take advantage of the precarious opportunity. Nonchalantly and unobserved, he had placed his black velvet case of diamonds inside Xen's tote bag, on top of another case of diamonds she had been contracted to carry.

Paulo had sincerely apologized for his clumsiness. Luckily, neither of them was injured. He helped Xen stand to her feet. It was quite an embarrassing moment. Nevertheless, they had shared a kind smile.

Xen had assured Paulo that she was okay, content that everything was fine. What she hadn't realized is that an extra case of diamonds was in her possession. Paulo had successfully stashed the cursed Almasi Ya Kifo stones with her.

Xen boarded the flight with the other passengers. The door to the jetway closed. The United Airlines Boeing 747 pushed off the gate, right on schedule. As the aircraft slowly moved away, Paulo walked close to the large terminal windows. He watched the beautiful jumbo jet taxi and takeoff, headed for Italy.

Then Paulo took his flight to Las Vegas.

· · · · ● ● ● · · ·

INSIDE THE TROPICANA lobby, Paulo stretches and yawns. He shakes his head and rolls his eyes, recalling how he clumsily smacked right into the pretty blonde transporter, bumping her off her feet. *Glad she was okay. And she never saw me place the diamonds in her purse.*

Yes indeed, Paulo needs a breather. He quietly turns the pages of the newspaper and starts to read an article about the Aladdin Resort, located nearby. He reads about the resort having some financial troubles of late.

"Mr. Pineda." Suddenly, the front desk lady calls out his name. "Sir, your room is ready now." She smiles as Paulo gets up and approaches her. "We apologize for the wait." She hands him the room key.

"Oh, that's okay." Paulo smiles in return.

"It's been so busy with Elton John being in town."

"Oh." Paulo recalls seeing the iconic artist's face glowing on the MGM Grand's gigantic digital marquee across the street.

Paulo makes his way through the crowd of people checking into the hotel and walks to the elevators. There he finds more people standing around, some with luggage, others holding souvenir alcoholic drinks of some kind. He hears their conversations. Everyone is making plans to meet up and be somewhere tonight. Paulo also has somewhere to be later, as well. He smiles. He can't wait to see Karen tonight. Karen and Paulo have worked together at the Megabuster video store the past three years. Although she is his boss at work, they are very good friends. Paulo has been seriously admiring her for some time now.

Paulo makes his way to his room and settles in. After counting his money, $3,450 Paulo lies down to take a nap. He stares at the ceiling, thinking. *I wonder where my lucky diamonds are right now.*

ALSO BY MAURY K. DOWNS

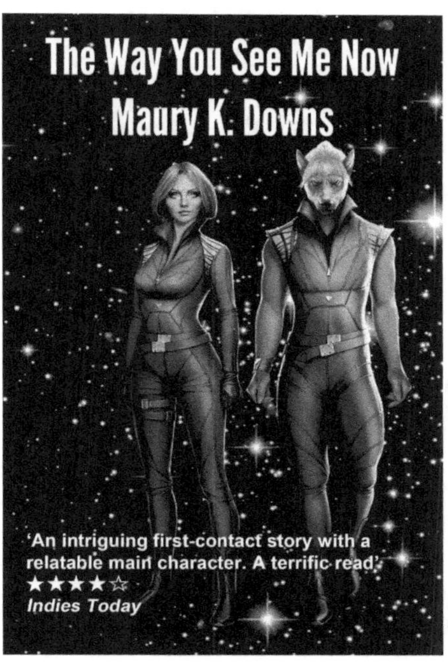

Aliens make a stealth landing late at night. They possess a unique capability never seen before. The mission becomes compromised when Brian discovers their presence. The aliens confront him, but he's unharmed. The aliens decide to continue with the mission and solicit Brian's help. Will they complete their important mission? Only destiny knows.